THE WEIRDEST,
MOST WONDERFUL ZOO
IN THE WORLD

Menagerie Dan's Monster Zoo: The Spotty Fingersnitch
A Picture Corgi 0 552 523984

Designed and produced by
Genesis Productions Limited
30 Great Portland Street, London W1

First published in Great Britain 1986

Picture Corgi Books are published by
Transworld Publishers Limited
61–63 Uxbridge Road, Ealing, London W5 5SA

Printed and bound in Hong Kong by
Mandarin Offset Marketing (H.K.) Ltd.

The Spotty Fingersnitch

John Cameron

A PICTURE CORGI

One day Dan set off to town to buy a fresh supply of food for the Monster Zoo.

He hadn't gone very far when he was stopped by a huge traffic jam. Cars and buses and lorries were all mixed up, hooting and honking, and nobody could move in any direction.

It didn't take long for Dan to see what was causing all the trouble. All the traffic lights had been stolen!

Dan thought hard. 'I know only one creature that would steal traffic lights ... but I can't remember its name!'

The following day he got into the truck to go to town to fetch some hay. After a few minutes he ran into an enormous pile of rubbish in the road. Someone had tipped all the rubbish out of the dustbins and taken them away.

'Pooh, what a pong!' said Dan, holding his nose. 'Now there's only one animal in the world that would steal all the dustbins in the town ... but I can't for the life of me remember what it's called!'

Next day Dan had to go to town again, to get a load of coal for heating the Zoo. He hadn't driven very far when he came upon a mountain of false teeth!

'Good grief!' said Dan. 'There's definitely only one creature that would steal all the false teeth in the town, and it's a ... it's a ... Fingersnitch! That's what it is!'

'Right, then,' said Dan. 'Tonight I'll set a trap to catch it.'

That night Dan looked in his big red book about monster-catching and found out that Fingersnitches will steal just about anything. They can't help it. They especially like shiny things, or anything that lights up.

Dan decided to set up his glue trap, baited with something really tasty – a lovely bright new torch.

He was just getting settled in for the night beside his trap, when out of the corner of his eye he saw a slithery yellow hand grabbing his sandwiches from his bag!

'Here, you!' cried Dan. 'Get your thieving hands off my sandwiches!' And he shot out to catch the Fingersnitch. But Dan forgot all about the trap, and he ran splat into the gooey glue. The Fingersnitch not only made off with Dan's sandwiches – it took the torch as well.

It took ages for Dan to get himself unstuck. When he did he stomped off back to the Zoo, determined to catch the Fingersnitch with a better trap the following day.

Dan's second trap was one of the oldest in his big red book. He dug a large, deep hole with very steep sides. Then he began to cover it over with leaves and branches to hide it. When the Fingersnitch came along, attracted by a shiny new dustbin, it would fall into the hole.

Dan was too busy covering the trap to notice a wiggly yellow hand making its way towards his wellies!

Suddenly the Fingersnitch jumped out in front of him ... wearing his wellies!

'Stop! Give me my wellies back!' yelled Dan, and he ran forward to catch the Fingersnitch. He forgot about the hole, crashed through the branches and fell right into it.

The Fingersnitch ran off with the dustbin and Dan's wellies. It was a long time before Dan managed to scramble out. All scratched and covered with mud, he limped barefoot back to the Zoo to think of yet another kind of trap.

The day after, Dan tried his patent treacle gun. He set it up in a clearing and aimed it at a brand-new set of false teeth.

'No Fingersnitch could resist those!' he thought.

What Dan didn't see was a slippery yellow hand sneaking towards the gun!

Sploosh! Quick as lightning the Fingersnitch turned the gun round and splattered Dan with gallons and gallons of squidgy black treacle! Needless to say, the false teeth were gone by the time Dan got up.

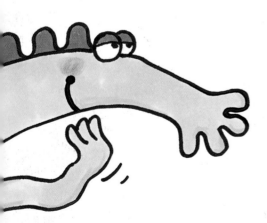

He had to have a hot bath and wash all his clothes. Then he sat down in his library with his big red monster book. 'There must be something I've missed,' he thought as he studied the chapter about Fingersnitches.

Sure enough, there at the bottom of the page was a clue. 'Fingersnitches are very stubborn. They won't let go of anything they've stolen, no matter what happens.'

'Now then,' said Dan. 'I think I've got an idea. Six wiggly arms, two legs and a wiggly nose. That means I'll need nine goldfish bowls for the perfect Fingersnitch trap!'

So the following morning Dan set out nine goldfish bowls with a shiny red apple in each, and sat back to wait for the Fingersnitch. Sure enough the Fingersnitch couldn't resist the apples, and a slithery yellow hand squirmed into a goldfish bowl to take one.

But it couldn't get the apple out without letting go.

Being very stubborn it wouldn't let go, no matter what.
It tried another apple and then another, until there was
a goldfish bowl stuck on every wriggling limb.

'Gotcha!' cried Dan.

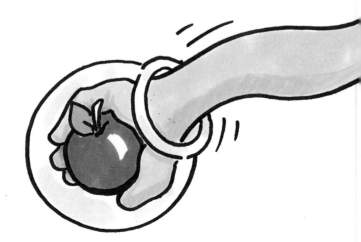

All Dan had to do now was snap some handcuffs on the Fingersnitch, smash the goldfish bowls and lead it back to the Zoo.

Dan put the Fingersnitch in a special snitchproof cage with a big sign on it telling people to stand back because it would pick their pockets. And that's where the Fingersnitch is today – safely under lock and key in the Monster Zoo...

Or is it?

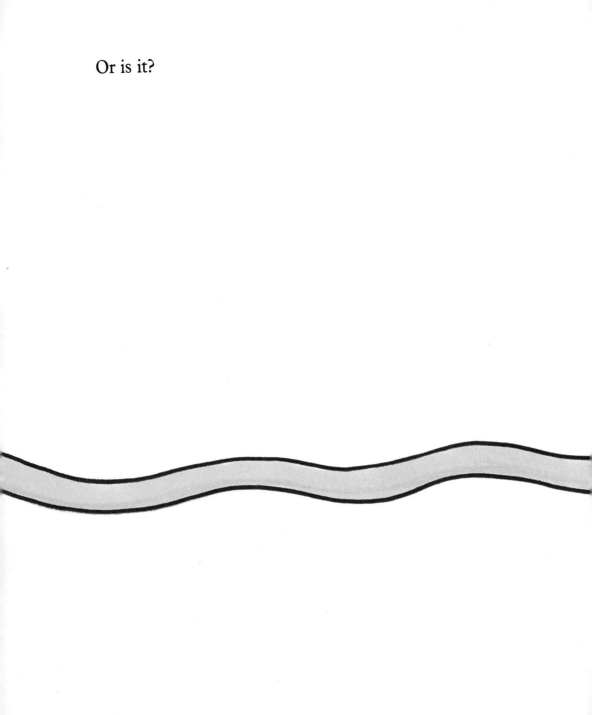

Other books in the Monster Zoo series include:

THE SMELLY PONGEROOS
THE GREAT BAMBOOZLE BIRD
THE ENORMOUS BLOB